ANNO'S SPAIN

MITSUMASA ANNO

PHILOMEL BOOKS
NEW YORK

Other Books by Mitsumasa Anno
Published by Philomel Books:

ANNO'S JOURNEY

ANNO'S U.S.A.

ANNO'S MYSTERIOUS MULTIPLYING JAR

L.C. Number: 2003107681

ISBN 0-399-24238-4
1 3 5 7 9 10 8 6 4 2
First Impression

A Note about Mitsumasa Anno and His Journey

The image one has of Mitsumasa Anno—moving wordlessly through the country-side of England or Italy or America with his peaked hat and his faithful horse—is a true one. Curious about the world around him since he was a child, Anno has been both an artist and a traveler all of his life. He remembers seeing the ocean for the first time at the age of ten and wondering about the countries beyond it. It was in 1963 that he first visited Europe with sketchbook and camera in hand. He rented a car and simply drove in a leisurely way from one end of a country to the other, stopping in a plaza or by the side of the road, taking out his small folding chair, and sketching whatever drew him to the scene.

He particularly likes to discover the details of a place, what makes it unique, be it a historical event or an architectural masterpiece, a place made famous by a piece of art, a story, or a person. Anno frequently follows people he knows or admires to their village or a place important to them. Thus, in his visit to Spain, he visited the ancient town of Toledo, where the artist El Greco lived; he made this drawing his book jacket.

He also visited and sketched the battlefield of Guadalajara because he "adored" the work of cellist Pablo Casals, who had fought there in the Spanish civil war. He visited Guernica in the Basque region, the bombing of which Pablo Picasso portrayed in his famous painting of the same name.

Two favorite artists of Anno, Joan Miró and Antoni Tàpies, were both born in Barcelona. Miró died in 1983, but Anno met Tàpies on this trip: he considered it "the chance of a life-time." Barcelona has a prominent place in his book.

The beach that appears in the beginning of this book was modeled after the beach at Cadaques, for "the great artist Salvador Dalí was born in Figueres, just north of Cadaques."

Not all of the people that Anno wanted to celebrate were flesh and blood, nor artists. He could "not think of Spain" without thinking of the fictional hero Don Quixote, and, to Anno, *Carmen* and bullfighting were primary elements of Spanish culture. He recalled scenes from his "favorite opera" when he drew the pages depicting Seville and Chincon.

Festivals, an integral part of Spanish life, needed to be celebrated, so Anno visited and sketched the Feria de Sevilla (Pilgrimage of Mother Mary) and the Fiesta de San Fermín (Bull Run in Pamplona). A third festival, Las Fallas de Valencia, he did not depict, as it takes place during the night.

The secluded country village of La Alberca "was quite impressive." He visited a Roman ruin that he had sketched on a previous trip, only to find that it had been torn down in the intervening years. Infuriated, he made a complaint to the mayor, who informed him that the previous ruin had been built by a British filmmaker as a scenery set!

Andalucía in southern Spain, a region that once flourished with Islamic culture, was of great interest to Anno. Five hundred years had passed since King Boabdil left the Spanish city of Alhambra "in indignation," but "incredibly," Anno still found hints and traces of his Islamic influence.

It had been pointed out to Anno that the whitewashed walls seen throughout the La Mancha and Andalucía regions are similar to those in the Suzhou region of China. "Indeed, I agree," Anno writes. He feels it is impossible not to think that these two parts of the world had some sort of cultural exchange in the past.

Anno visited Santiago de Compostela Cathedral, to which it was an old tradition for Christians from Germany and France to traverse the Pyrenees in a pilgrimage. Anno wondered how these travelers felt, finally reaching this sacred place after their arduous journey.

Anno knew that it would be impossible to draw the whole of Spain and its historical and literary moments, but, like the travelers on their long walk, "when I finished this picture book, I felt as if I had reached the holy place, too."

In this celebration of historical, architectural, and human moments, Anno blends the liveliness of the present with the power and beauty of the past. He has mentioned many of the allusions in this book, but he has left many others to be discovered by the curious as well as the adventurous and the knowledgeable. The journey now becomes the reader's.